ANTI-VAX ABCs

By J.D. McKay
Illustrated by Coffin Nachtmahr

Cover design and layout by Andra McKay
Illustrations by Coffin Nachtmahr

The Author is not to be held responsible for the actions of people with no sense of humour. Anyone objecting to the content of this work of satire is directed to comment publicly on a blog or social media including a link to where to purchase the book rather than emailing the author who reserves the right to mock your indignation.

J.D. McKay
Visit my website at www.jdmckay.com

Printed in the United States of America

First Printing: December 2019
J.D. McKay

ISBN-978-1-9991887-5-7

To everyone out there who lacks a sense of humor, or just plain lacks sense.
May you acquire both.

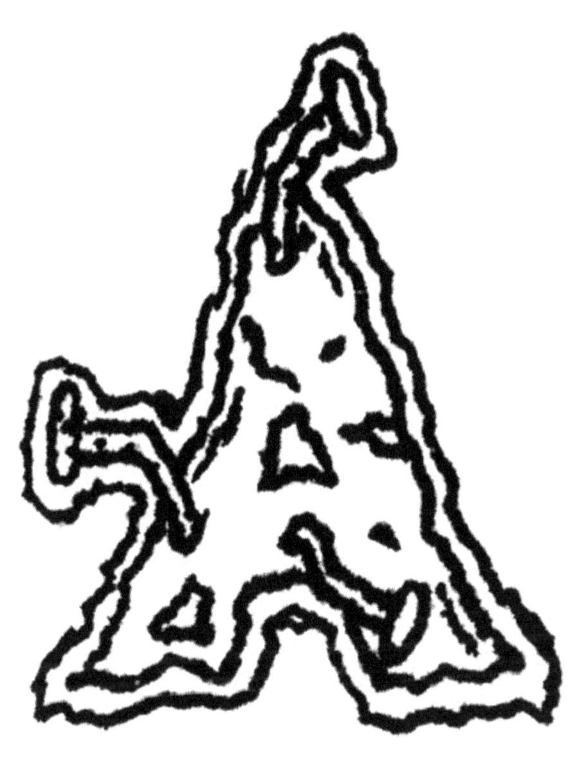

Andy, Age 9
was born with a gift
a passion for oceans
if you get my drift

A machine to clean water
he might have invented,
had the agony of TETANUS
only relented.

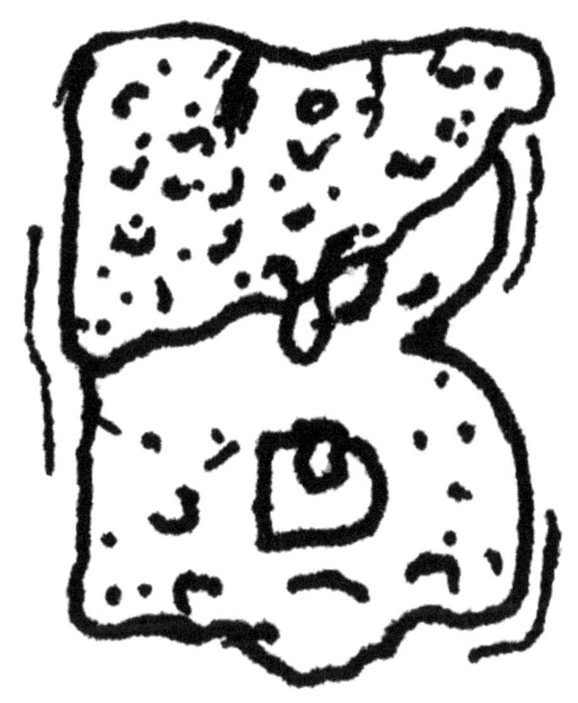

Beth, age 6
a botanist to be.
could she save the rainforests?
we'll never see

HEPATITUS B
sadly stunted her learning
acute liver failure
is never discerning.

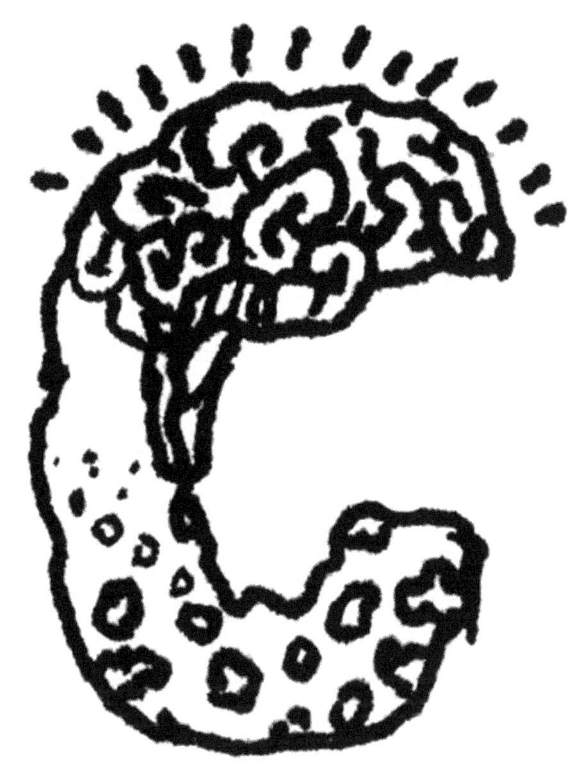

Charlie, age 16
worked writing letters
campaigning for changes
to make lives better

Their passion for politics
would have brought change
but MENINGOCOCCAL bacteria
left Charlie quite deranged.

Donald, age 7
travelled the world
his parents built houses
for poor boys and girls

Their plans were derailed
by the need to hover
CHOLERA left Don runny
from one end to the other,

Erica, 32
thought she was fine
a life free of illness
'til just the right time

7 months pregnant
CHICKEN POX from a friend
Erica's unborn child
met an untimely end

Flower, age 8
loved to play lacrosse
from goalie to forward
she was the boss

A cleat to the head
MENINGITIS found a way
into a coma she fell
for the rest of her days

Geri, age 6
the actress to be
would travel the world
oh the sights she would see

An audition for a role
to star in a movie
PERTUSSIS led to seizures
so very un-groovy

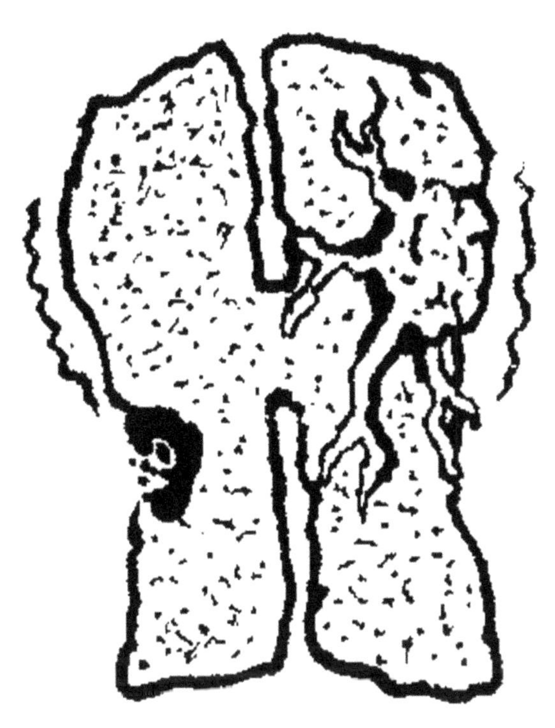

Horace, age 3
was his mom's little man
he was coddled and pampered
like a star in a band

Family went overseas
some culture to gain
but TYPHOID caught hold
hard-boiling his brain

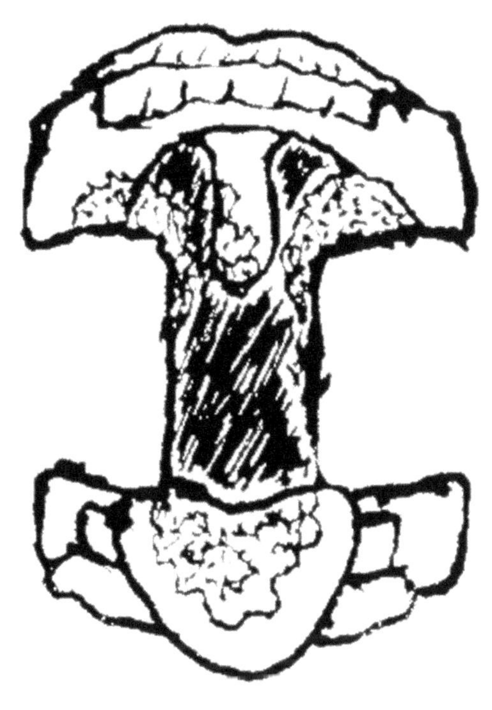

Iris, age 16
a diva was she
singing opera and jazz
with clear voiced esprit

To Thailand she went
to tour with a play
DIPTHERIA's nerve damage
stole her voice away

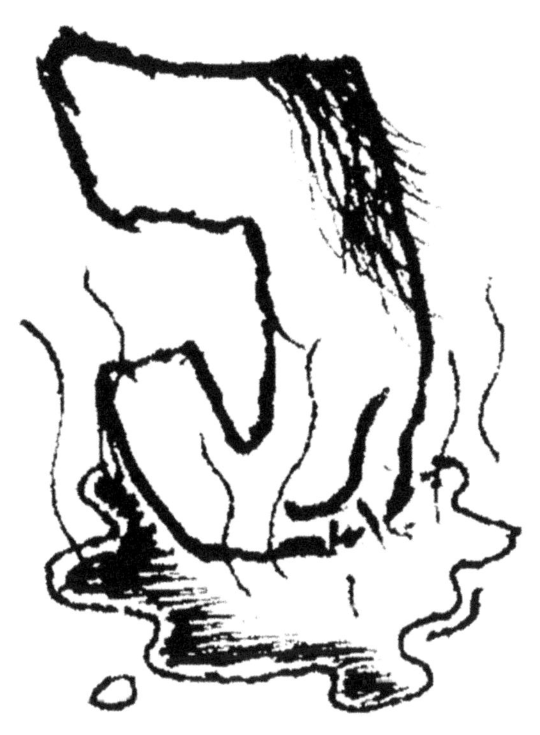

Jayden, age 13
ate like a teen
junk food and pop
at levels unseen

ROTAVIRUS struck
left Jay's guts a disaster
a diet of vegetables
and plain rice thereafter

Kerry, age 16
newly in love
in the woods with her boyfriend
the bright stars above

Youthful foolishness struck
he was sadly untested
HPV passed along
left her uterus arrested

Logan, age 8
loved to play with his friends
through forest or field
they would run end to end

Influenza struck hard
his running days ended
from BACTERIAL PNEUMONIA
his lungs never mended

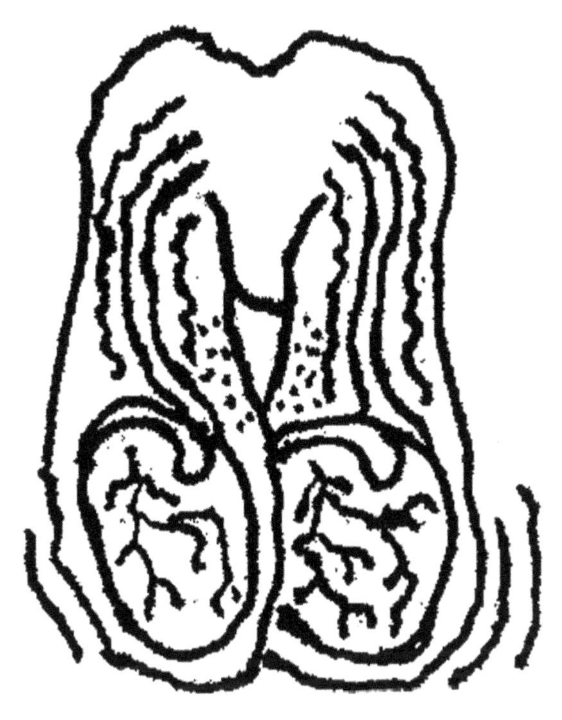

For Mason, age 19
a big family was the dream
the girl next door
filled his eyes with that gleam

Before he could propose
to his childhood bestie
the MUMPS struck him down
and devoured his testes

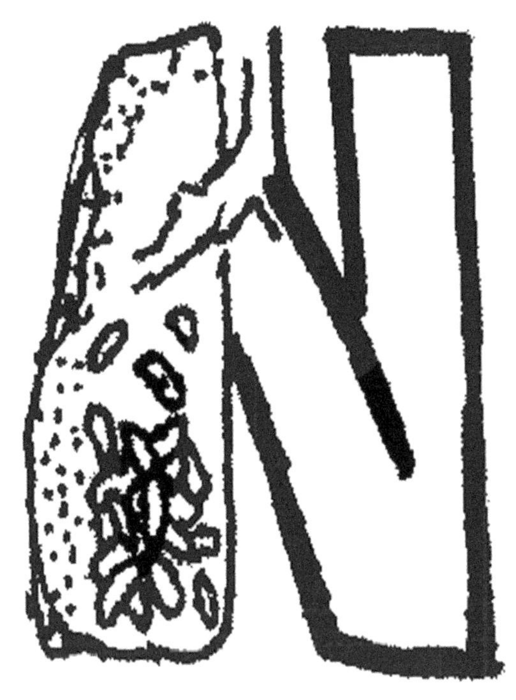

Nadine, age 18
had a plan for her life
a high level mediator
she planned to end strife

She traveled the world
learning culture and history
TUBERCULOSIS ate her lungs
her death was quite gory

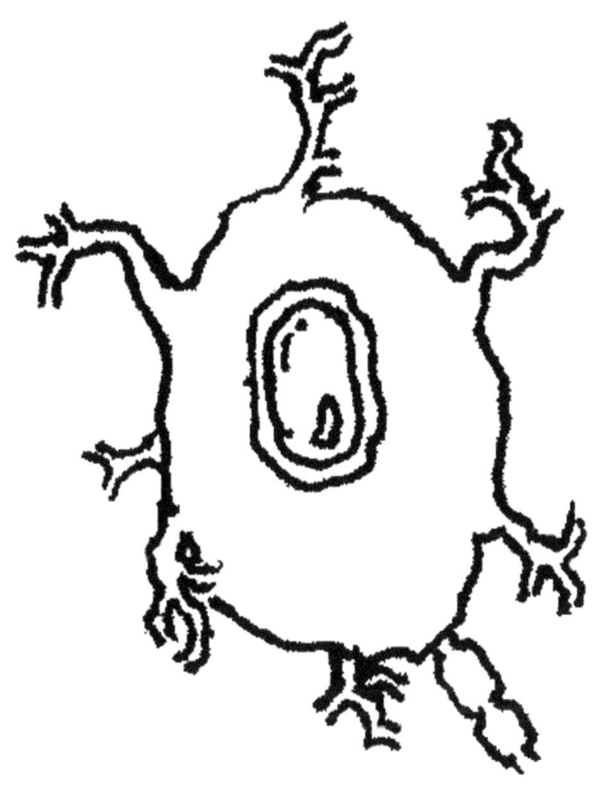

Oscar, age 5
in the town of Flint
was an odd little fellow
skin a yellowish tint

POLIO struck
the priest prayed and blessed
now he breathes by machine
his nerve cells quite a mess

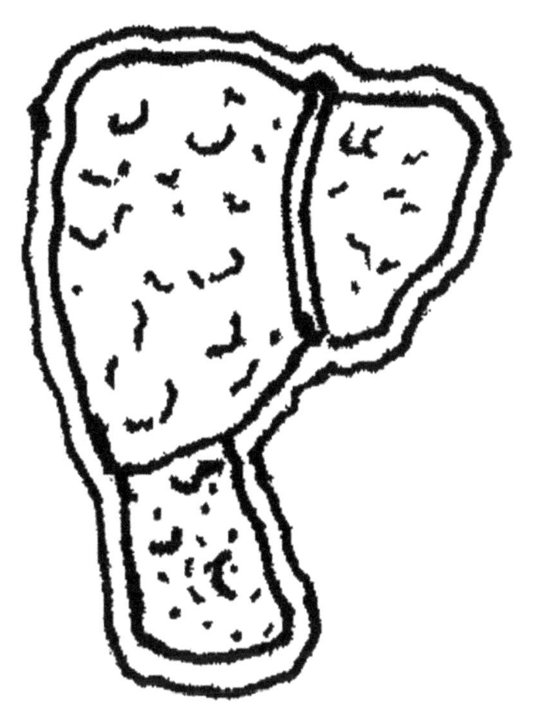

Penn, age 16
was tired all the time
their parents thought nothing
all teenagers whine

Acute liver failure
HEP A was at fault
a transplant-shortened lifespan
brought Penn's dreams to a halt

Quinlan, age 3
was a cheerful young man
his mom raised him alonc
on the road in a van

SHINGLES severe
left mom blind and in pain
poor Quin wandered off
never heard from again

Rachel, age 4
adored kisses and hugs
almost as much
as collecting small bugs

One sneeze from a classmate
and she caught HIB
SEPTICEMIA took hold
left her dead as could be

Stewie, age 7
was left all alone
to live with an aunt
very far from his home

Both parents went hiking
in Europe for fun
TICK-BORNE ENCEPHALITIS
Stew's parent count: none

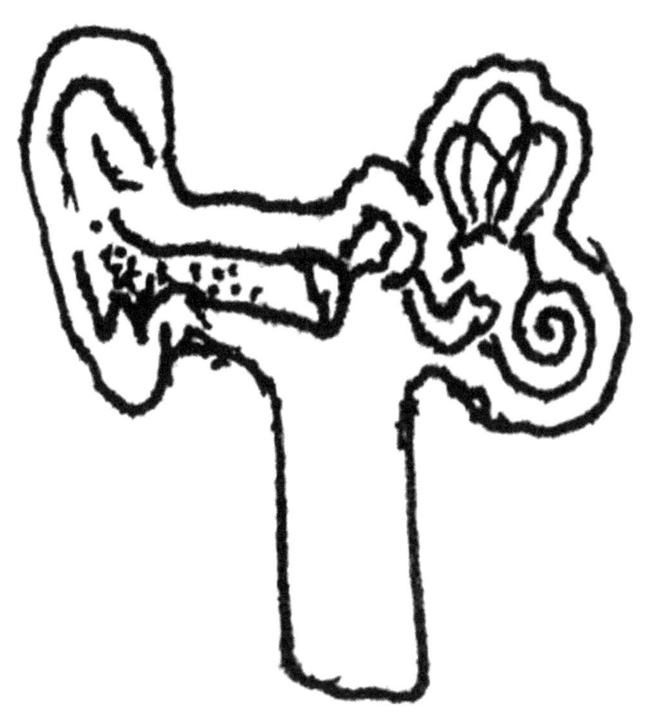

Taylor, age 5
they loved music the most
a future composer
their parents did boast

A random sneeze
from someone tissue-bereft
PNEUMOCCCOCAL DISEASE
left Taylor permanently deaf

Ulric, age 12
his dad hunted for sport
trips into the woods
instead of fancy resorts

A cranky racoon bite
transmitted RABIES
he fell into a coma
then poor Ulric was gone

Veronica, age 8
family trip to Brazil
she caught a wee bug
and felt a bit ill

She got somewhat better
then a whole lot worse
YELLOW FEVER unchecked
sent her home in a hearse

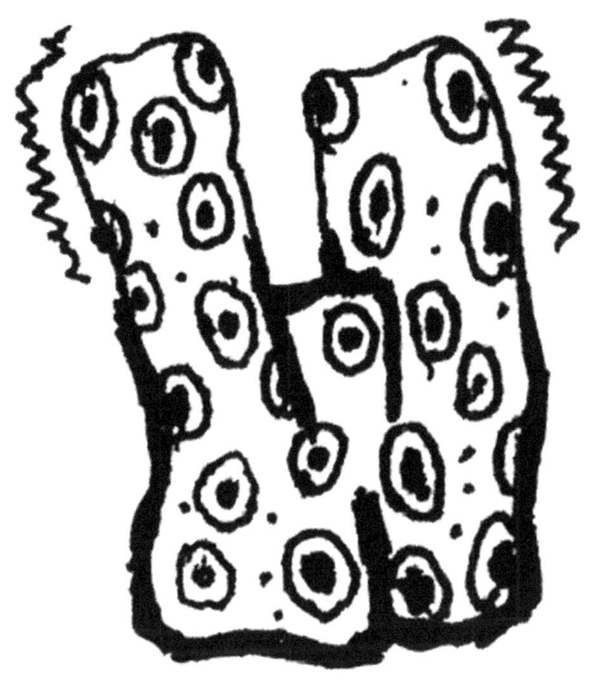

Wilma, age 9
was a terrible tease
her friends found her fickle
moods changed with the breeze

Her inflated ego
soon met its match
MEASLES swelled up her brain
leaving thoughts hard to catch

Xan, age 8
was a brave young man
an archaeologist's son
his family visited Iran

MALARIA struck
left the father quite weak
and poor Xan in a coma
unable to speak

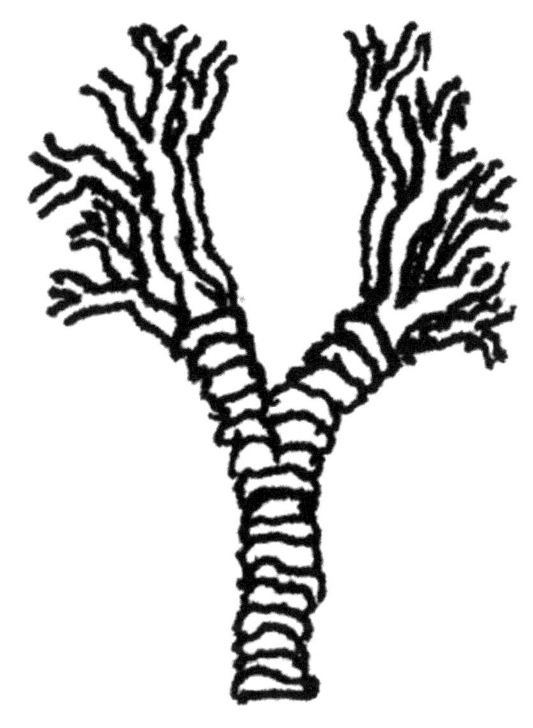

Yohan, age 3
was a bright smiling baby
his perfect brown hair
was movie star wavy

INFLUENZA struck hard
triggering asthma unknown
he died in his sleep
scared, breathless, and alone

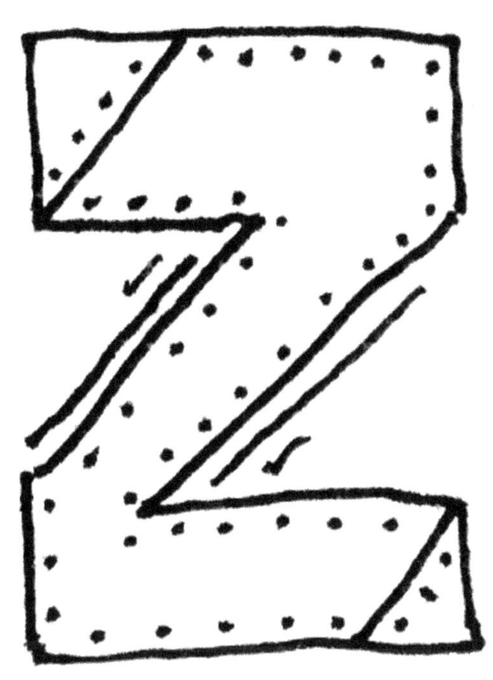

Zane, age 16
in court sued and won
to stop misinformed parents
from neglecting their son

He got his vaccinations
as a sensible person would
and lived a full life
finding joy where he could

Join the madness by signing up at jdmckay.com.

You'll receive a **free copy** of The Duck: How to make THEM Pay – A Survivalists guide to the Coming Duckpocalypse.

Newsletters go out about once a month with release updates and the occasional free story.

Here's a bonus Limerick to prepare you for your free guide.

> There once was a man from Kentucky
> Who's avian farm was just ducky
> Then Duckpocalypse day came
> Humans all die the same
> Now the farm...

The ending of that limerick is too gruesome even for THIS book, so we'll just leave it at that.

One final note.

Reviews help potential readers decide to make a purchase. Please head to Amazon and leave a quick review. I look forward to reading them all!

About the Author

J.D. McKay is a recreational madman. He uses his ADHD as a tactical weapon on a daily basis to encourage critical thinking, creativity, and general enjoyment of life.
He dislikes Ducks. Very much.

About the Illustrator

Coffin Nachtmahr is a professional...Coffin Nachtmahr. One could describe him as somewhere between an artist and a real live piece of art.

Where to find us

If you enjoyed this book, head over to www.jdmckay.com to see what else I'm up to and to join my mailing list for updates on future releases!

Find Coffin on Facebook being...Coffin.

www.ingramcontent.com/pod-product-compliance
Ingram Content Group UK Ltd.
Pitfield, Milton Keynes, MK11 3LW, UK
UKHW020136250726
13967UKWH00002B/694